ARCHIE'S
HOLIDAY

for
Charlie
X

Bloomsbury Publishing, London, New Delhi, New York and Sydney

First published in Great Britain in 2013 by Bloomsbury Publishing Plc
50 Bedford Square, London, WC1B 3DP

This paperback edition first published in 2014

Text and illustrations copyright © Domenica More Gordon 2013
The moral right of the author/illustrator has been asserted

A CIP catalogue record for this book is available from the British Library

ISBN 978 1 4088 2932 5 (HB)
ISBN 978 1 4088 2931 8 (PB)

1 3 5 7 9 10 8 6 4 2

Printed in China by C & C Offset Printing Co Ltd, Shenzhen, Guangdong

All papers used by Bloomsbury Publishing are natural, recyclable products
made from wood grown in well-managed forests. The manufacturing processes
conform to the environmental regulations of the country of origin

www.bloomsbury.com
www.domenicamoregordon.com

ARCHIE'S
HOLIDAY

Domenica More Gordon

BLOOMSBURY

LONDON NEW DELHI NEW YORK SYDNEY

La la la
la la la
laaaa

HAIL?
RAIN?
SNOW?
HURRICANES?
LIGHTNING?
THUNDER?
WATERPROO
LONG, THICK, WOOLL
MORE SOCKS!
YIKES!
FREEZIN
NO!

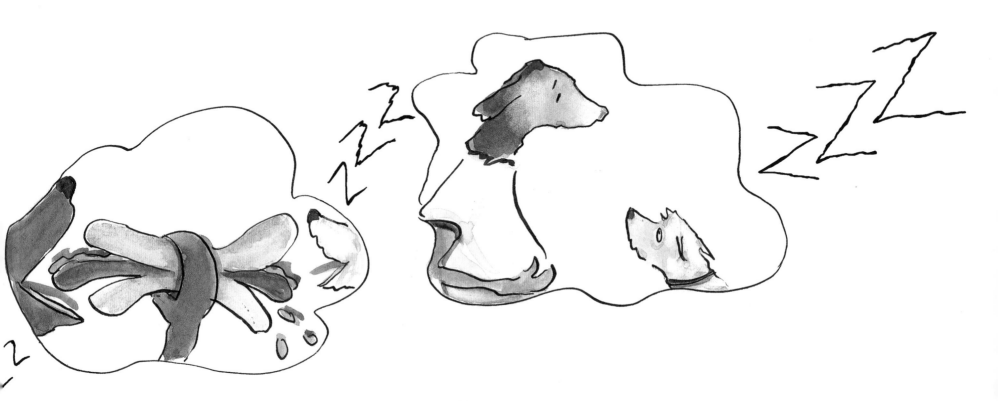

PILLS FOR EVERYTHING!

BLUE PILLS, RED PILLS, LOZENGES

ALL POSSIBLE TYPES OF CREAM!

JELLY FISH STING CREAM

SMALL PILLS

BIG PILLS

ICE PACKS

ANTI SNAKE VENOM STUFF

MORE CREAM

PHEW!

ALLERGIES?

HELP!

THAT'S BETTER!

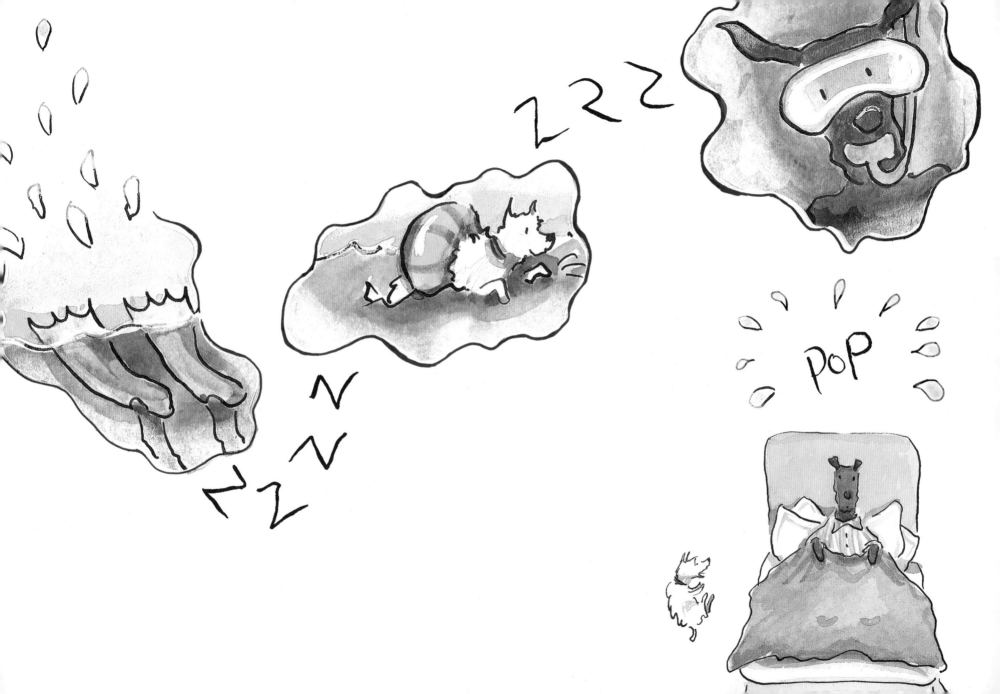

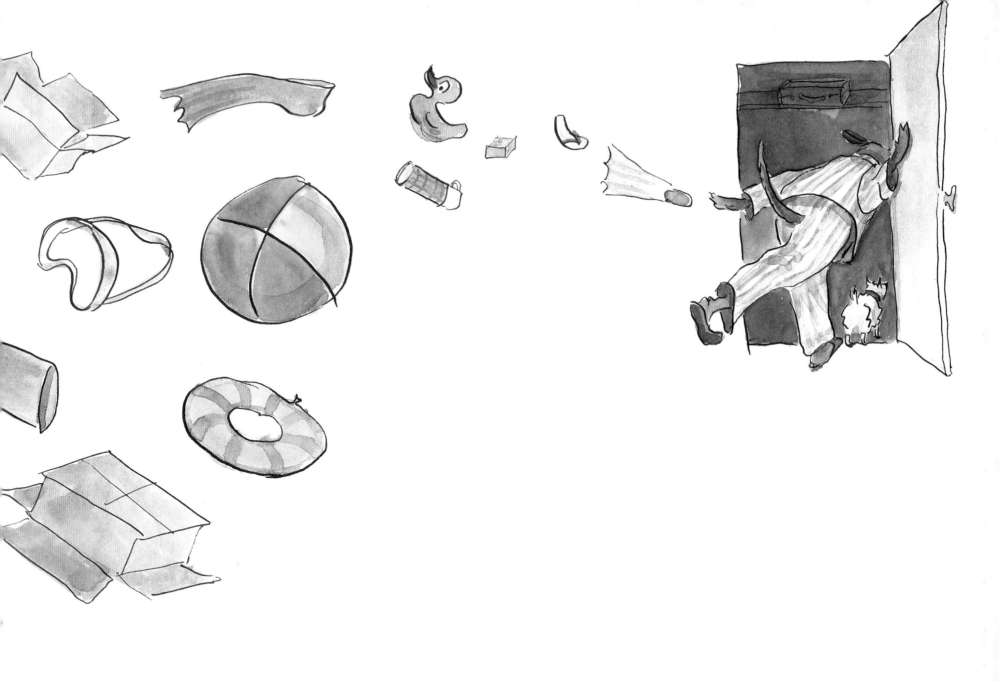

DECKCHAIRS × 2
BLOW UP LOCH NESS MONSTER
SHARK CAGE!
SPADE
ARMBANDS
FRYING PAN
SWIMMING CAPS + 2
EXTRA TRUNKS
SUBMARINE?
WETSUITS
PIRATE
? BAT
WINDSURFER
'THE WONDERFUL WORLD OF SHELLS'
WINDBREAKER
FAKE SHARK FIN
BARBEQUE BUCKET
'KNOW YOUR SEAWEED' BOOK
BEACH BAG
CANOE?
CRICKET BAT
SNORKELS + 2
FISHIN

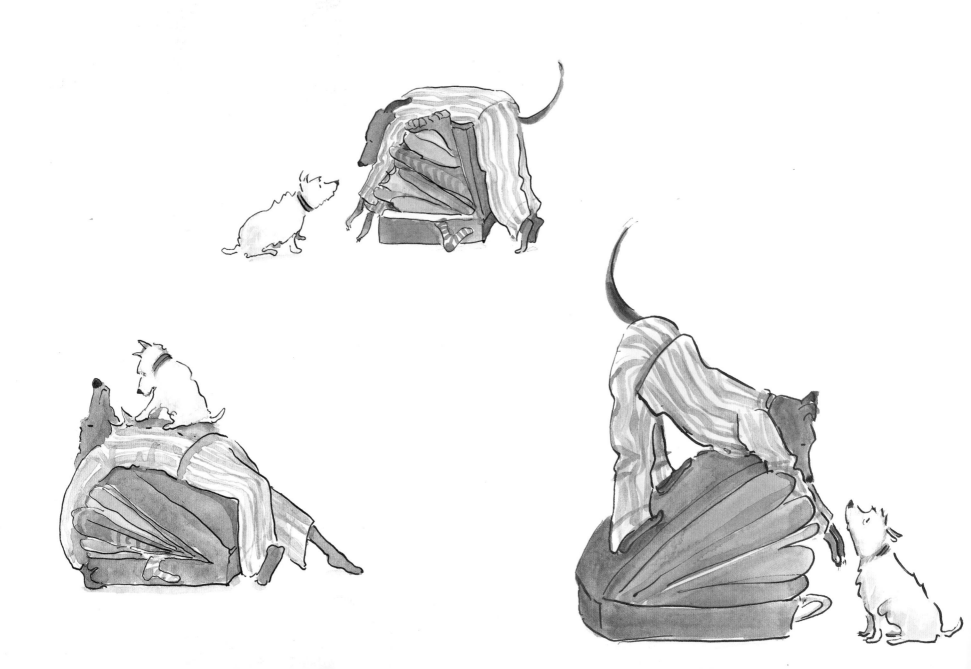

CREEEAK

BA

NG!

BARK
BARK
BARK

Pom de pom

Pom
pom
pom de
pom

"   "

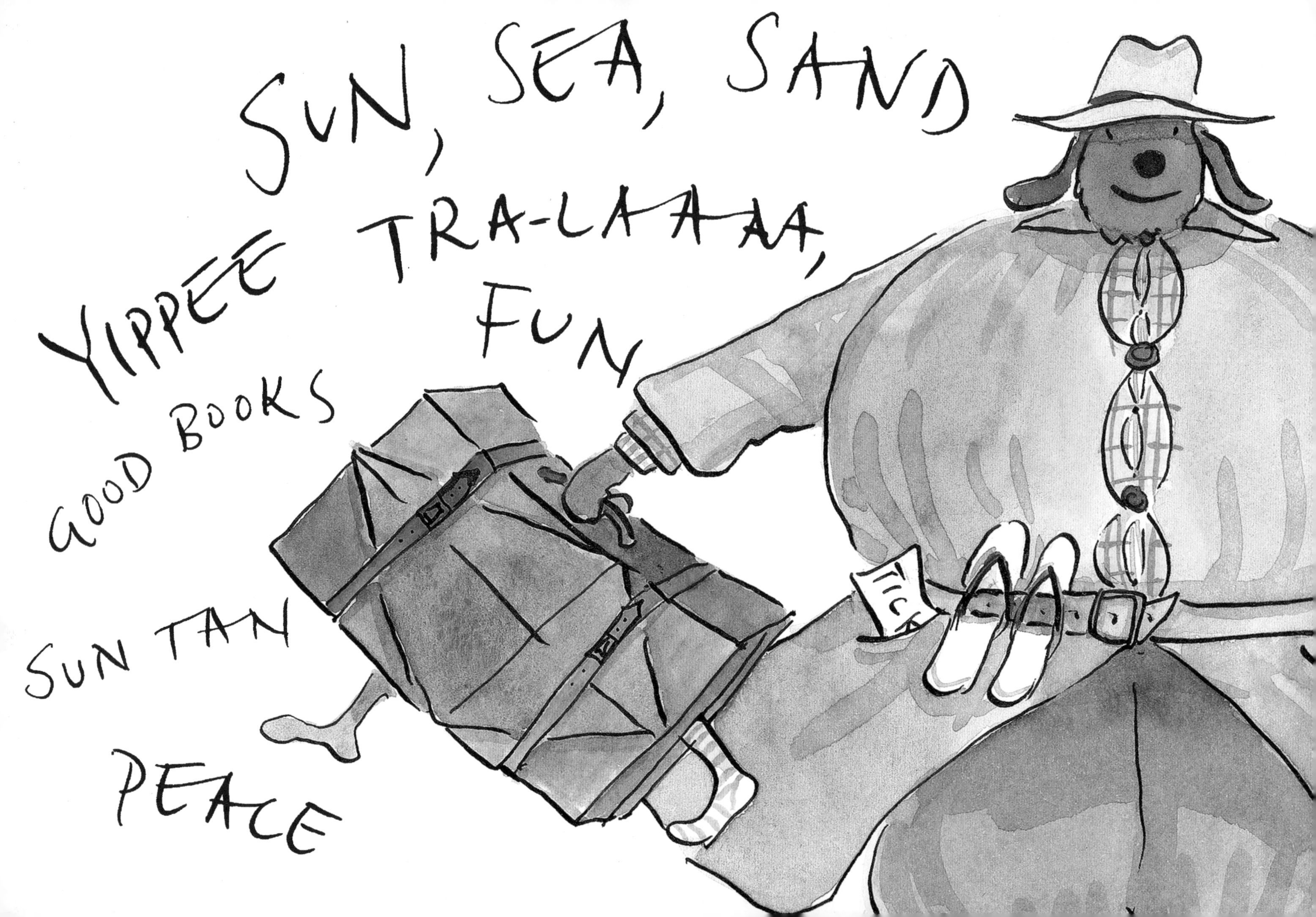
SUN, SEA, SAND
YIPPEE
TRA-LA-AAAA,
FUN
GOOD BOOKS
SUN TAN
PEACE

HERE WE COME!
HOORAY
WAHOO!
ICE CREAM
HOLIDAYS FOREVER!
NEW FRIENDS
NEW THOUGHTS
NEW ME!

Wish you were here!

ARCHIE x